MW01076878

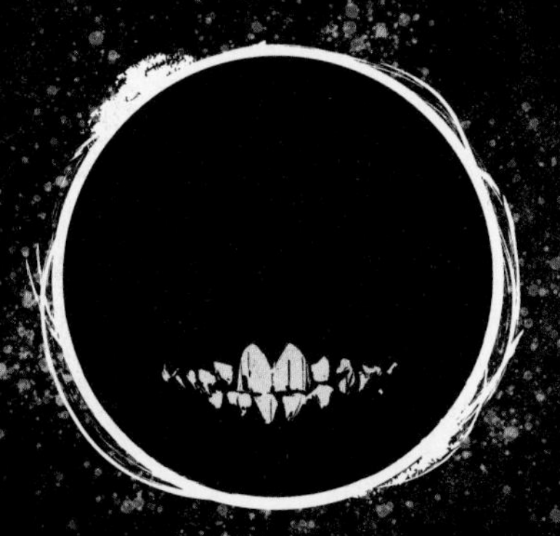

THE CLOSET

WRITTEN BY **JAMES TYNION IV**

ART BY **GAVIN FULLERTON**

COLORS BY **CHRIS O'HALLORAN**

LETTERS BY **TOM NAPOLITANO**

EDITED BY **GREG LOCKARD**

DESIGN BY **DYLAN TODD**

THE CLOSET

OCTOBER 2022. PUBLISHED BY IMAGE COMICS, INC.
Office of publication: PO BOX 14457, Portland, OR 97293.
For international rights, contact: foreignlicensing@imagecomics.com.
ISBN: 978-1-5343-2325-4

ONE

IT'S FUNNY.
I THOUGHT YOU MOVED TO LOS ANGELES OR SOMETHING LIKE A MONTH AGO.
PORTLAND. AND YOU'RE THINKING OF THE GOODBYE PARTY WE THREW FOR OUR FRIENDS A FEW WEEKS BACK.
MOVING VAN SHOWS UP IN THE MORNING.
I'M OUT ON A SUPPLY RUN AS WE GET THROUGH THE LAST-MINUTE PACKING.
NEEDED MORE PACKING TAPE.
TAKING THE LONG WAY HOME FROM THE STORE, I SEE.

I'M JUST GETTING IN THE WAY UP THERE. YOU KNOW? I GET ALL FLUSTERED, AND MAGGIE KNOWS EXACTLY WHERE SHE WANTS EVERYTHING.
THEN SHE TELLS ME AND I GET IT WRONG, AND THEN WE'RE SHOUTING AND NOBODY'S GETTING ANYTHING DONE.

MOVING'S STRESSFUL.
YEAH.

THIS WAY I'LL COME IN AT THE END AND TAPE EVERYTHING UP.

CAN'T BUILD BOXES WITHOUT TAPE, THOUGH.

YEAH. GUESS NOT.

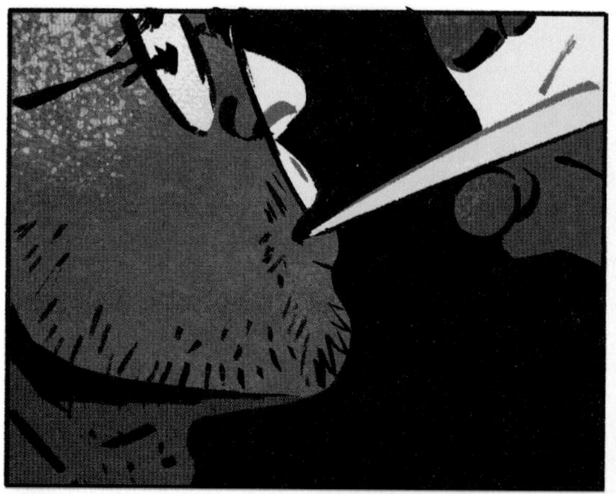

JUST ONE MORE, OKAY? I'LL SAY THE FIRST STORE I TRIED WAS OUT OF TAPE.
YOU'RE THE BOSS.

IT'S WILD PACKING THE PLACE UP. IT'S LIKE THERE'S THIS WHOLE OLD LIFE HIDING IN THE CORNERS OF THE PLACE.
THE PEOPLE WE WERE BEFORE WE GOT MARRIED. BEFORE WE HAD JAMIE.

I FOUND THIS BOX IN THE BACK OF THE HALL CLOSET. ALL THESE BOOKS I'D BEEN SHARING WITH THIS GIRL I WAS SEEING AGES AGO.
MAGGIE DIDN'T LIKE THAT.

I BET NOT. BUT YOU CAN'T HAVE GOTTEN IN TOO MUCH TROUBLE OVER HAVING A LIFE BEFORE HER.

IT'S MORE JUST THAT I SAID I GOT RID OF IT ALL AGES AGO, AND I THOUGHT I HAD. BUT I DIDN'T.
IT'S NOT THAT I HAD IT...IT'S THAT I SAID I DID SOMETHING AND DIDN'T.

THAT'S USUALLY HOW I GET IN TROUBLE.

LIKE I WAS SUPPOSED TO TALK TO THIS FRIEND OF MINE'S WIFE, WHO'S A CHILD PSYCHOLOGIST, ABOUT THESE NIGHTMARES JAMIE IS HAVING.
NIGHTMARES?

YEAH. CLASSIC STUFF. MONSTER IN THE CLOSET.

I KEEP TELLING MAGGIE THAT HE WON'T EVEN HAVE THE FUCKING CLOSET IN OREGON, SO IT'S POINTLESS TO MAKE A FUSS.
BUT I SAID I'D CALL AND I DIDN'T, AND I GOT IN TROUBLE.

UNICORN PISS.

WHAT?

THAT'S WHAT MY SISTER DOES WITH HER KID. SHE HAS A LITTLE SPRAY BOTTLE THAT SHE FILLS UP WITH WATER AND A LITTLE BIT OF LAVENDER SO IT SMELLS NICE.
GIVES A FEW SPRAYS UNDER THE BED EACH NIGHT, SAYING THAT IT'S LIKE DOGS MARKING TERRITORY. MONSTERS STAY AWAY FROM THE UNICORN PISS.

THAT'S INSANE.

I MEAN, I THINK IT'S MORE ABOUT TAKING THE FEAR SERIOUSLY. OTHERWISE, KIDS LEARN THAT THEY CAN'T GO TO THEIR PARENTS WITH ANY OF IT.

THAT'S WHAT SHE SAYS. I WOULDN'T KNOW. DON'T HAVE KIDS. I JUST GET TO BE THE FUN UNCLE. THROW THEM AROUND AND ALL THAT.
YEAH.

I DON'T KNOW. IT'LL BE BETTER OUT THERE. I GET TOO MUCH IN MY HEAD HERE IN THE CITY. TOO MANY GHOSTS OF MY OLD LIFE, YOU KNOW?

I SEE THESE FUCKING KIDS, AND I WISH I WAS STILL ONE OF THEM. SOMETIMES, ANYWAYS.

OUT THERE, I'LL BE ABLE TO FOCUS A BIT MORE. BE THERE IN THE RIGHT WAYS. SPRAY ALL THE CLOSETS WITH UNICORN PISS.

JUST ONE MORE AND THE CHECK, OKAY?

THIS ONE'S ON ME.
HAPPY TRAILS.

JESUS, THOM. REALLY?

THE FIRST STORE I WENT TO...
PLEASE. DON'T. I CAN SMELL.
OKAY.
CAN I TAPE ANYTHING UP?

DADDY?

HEY, BUDDY.

CAN...CAN I SLEEP WITH YOU TONIGHT?

SORRY, LITTLE GUY. MOM NEEDS ME TO STAY UP LATE TO FINISH PACKING.

BUT WE'RE GOING ON A ROAD TRIP TOMORROW, AND YOU CAN SLEEP WITH ME EVERY NIGHT, OKAY?

YEAH...
BUT...

HERE. WAIT A SECOND.

DO WE HAVE AN EMPTY SPRAY BOTTLE? LIKE AN OLD WINDEX?

WHAT? NO. OF COURSE NOT. WE DON'T EVEN HAVE REGULAR WINDEX. EVERYTHING IS PACKED UP.

SHIT. OKAY...

GLASS

SEE THIS? THIS IS UNICORN PISS.

NO.

IT IS. I PROMISE IT IS.

IT'S FROM THE SINK. I SAW.

COME ON. LET ME SHOW YOU HOW IT WORKS.

SEE, THE MONSTERS, THEY DON'T LIKE THE SMELL OF UNICORNS PEEING.
WHY?

IT'S LIKE DOGS. YOU KNOW HOW DOGS SNIFF FIRE HYDRANTS? MARK THEIR TERRITORY.
NO.

FUCK.
THAT'S A BAD WORD.
YEAH.

OKAY. YOU CAUGHT ME. THIS ISN'T UNICORN PISS. THIS IS WATER. BUT THERE'S NOTHING IN THE CLOSET, ALRIGHT?

SEE?

AND EVEN IF THERE WAS. THIS IS OUR LAST NIGHT IN THIS APARTMENT. TOMORROW WE START DRIVING AND WE WON'T EVER SEE THIS APARTMENT OR THAT CLOSET AGAIN.
THE MONSTER CAN BOTHER THE NEXT KID WHO LIVES IN THIS ROOM, OKAY?
I'M SCARED.
YOU'VE MADE IT THROUGH FOUR WHOLE YEARS IN THIS ROOM, AND YOU'RE STILL STANDING BECAUSE YOU'RE THE BRAVEST BOY I KNOW.
NOW GO TO SLEEP. WE'LL LEAVE THIS ALL BEHIND TOMORROW.

WHAT?

YOU CAN'T DO THAT, THOM.
WHAT?

YOU MADE IT MY FAULT THAT HE COULDN'T SLEEP WITH US. THAT'S NOT FAIR TO ME...IF YOU KEEP THAT UP, HE'S GOING TO INTERNALIZE ALL OF THAT.

SHIT. I'M SORRY, I DIDN'T THINK.
NO, YOU DIDN'T.

AND IS THIS FUCKING MASKING TAPE? ARE YOU KIDDING ME, THOM?

HEY. LET'S NOT DO THIS. IN A FEW DAYS WE'RE GOING TO BE IN A WONDERFUL HOUSE AND STARTING A WHOLE NEW LIFE TOGETHER.

THAT DOESN'T LET YOU OFF THE HOOK!

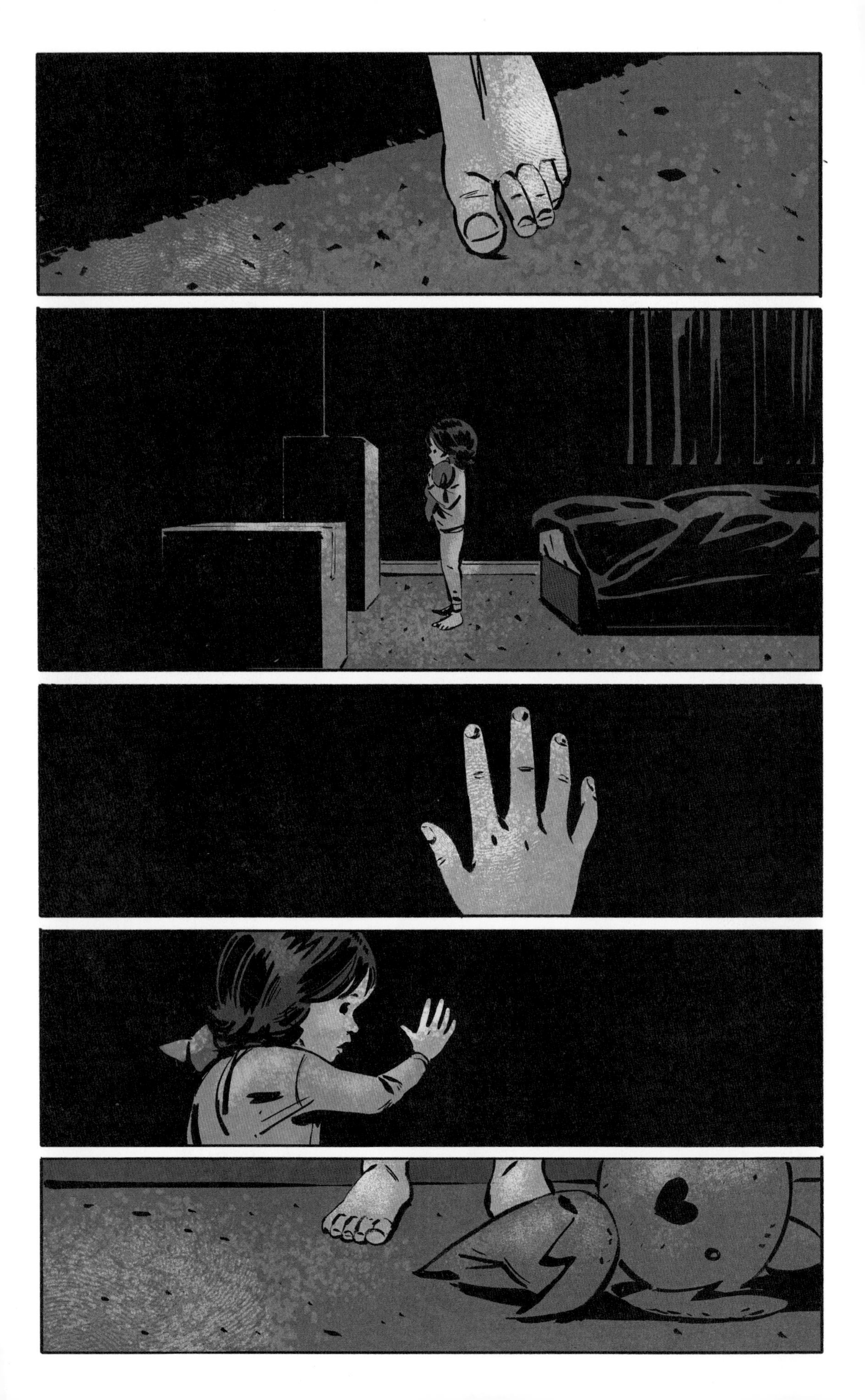

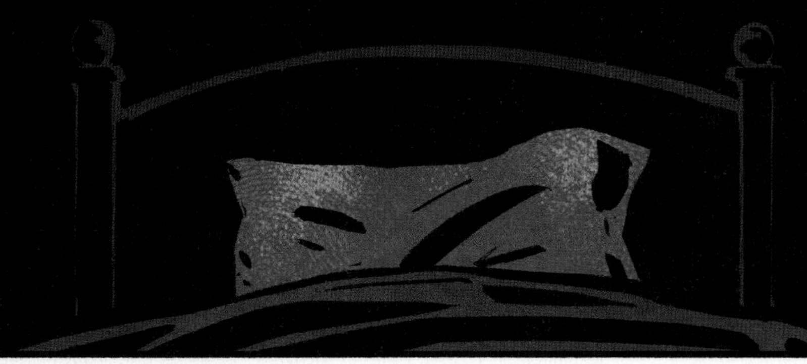

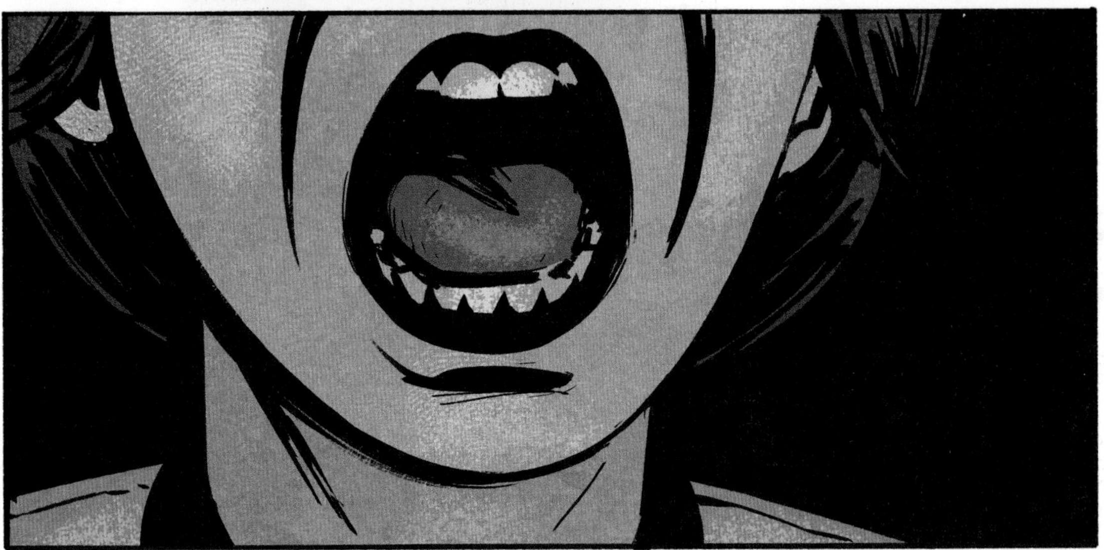

JAMIE! ARE YOU ALRIGHT?!

HEY, BUDDY. YOU'RE OKAY. YOU'RE OKAY.

HE'S COMING, TOO.

HEY, YOU JUST HAD A NIGHTMARE. IT'S OKAY. YOU CAN COME SLEEP IN OUR BED.

AND STARTING TOMORROW, YOU'LL NEVER HAVE TO SEE THAT CLOSET EVER AGAIN.

TO BE CONTINUED

TWO

HEY, BUDDY. I'M SORRY, OKAY?
I DIDN'T MEAN TO GET UPSET.
I KNOW.
WE DON'T HAVE TO TELL MOM, OKAY?
OKAY.

IS THIS A MOUNTAIN?
I GUESS IT MIGHT BE. NOT AS BIG AS THE ONES WE DROVE THROUGH A LITTLE WAYS BACK.
THAT WAS COOL, RIGHT?
THE TUNNELS THROUGH THE MOUNTAIN?
THIS IS PORTLAND?
NO. WE HAVE A FEW MORE DAYS UNTIL WE GET TO PORTLAND.
OH.

ARE THERE MOUNTAINS IN PORTLAND?
YEAH, BUDDY. LOTS OF MOUNTAINS.
THEY'RE KIND OF SCARY.
I KNOW, RIGHT? FILLED WITH BEARS AND ALL SORTS OF SCARY THINGS.
BUT WE'RE BRAVE, AREN'T WE?

OKAY, I THINK THIS IS IT.

YOU'RE LIKE THREE HOURS LATE, THOM.
IT WAS A NIGHTMARE GETTING OUT OF A CITY. WE'RE LUCKY IT'S STILL **THIS** EARLY.

JEAN MADE SOME DINNER A WHILE BACK. I CAN HEAT IT UP.
IT'S ALL GOOD. WE PICKED UP SOME MCDONALD'S ON THE ROAD.

WELL, THEN I'LL JUST HEAT UP MINE.

SHIT. YOU WAITED...
WE CAN STILL--

BUDDY, YOU WANT TO HAVE SECOND DINNER?
NO.

IT'S FINE. AS LONG AS I GET TO SEE MY LITTLE PAL HERE. LOOK HOW BIG HE IS!

YOU REMEMBER DADDY'S FRIEND MACK, DON'T YOU, JAMIE?
OF COURSE YOU DO.
I DON'T KNOW...

IT'S COOL, MAN. I HAVEN'T SEEN HIM SINCE HE WAS HALF THIS SIZE.
GIVE ME HIS BAG. WE CAN SET HIM UP IN THE GUEST ROOM.

YEAH, JUST A SECOND.

OH, SHIT.

WHAT'S WRONG?
I THINK HIS BAG GOT PACKED BY THE MOVERS. IT'S NOT IN THE CAR.

JESUS, THOM.

IT'S OKAY. HE CAN JUST PUT ON ONE OF MY T-SHIRTS.
DOES HE HAVE A TOOTHBRUSH, ANYTHING LIKE THAT?
FUCK.

MAGGIE IS GOING TO KILL ME.

ALL RIGHT, BOYS. TIME FOR A WAL-MART RUN.

COME ON, WE'VE BEEN IN THE CAR FOR ALMOST EIGHT HOURS.
HE CAN SLEEP IN A T-SHIRT AND GO A NIGHT WITHOUT BRUSHING.

YOU WANT TO SKIP BRUSHING YOUR TEETH TONIGHT, JAMIE?

YEAH!

SEE?

JEAN'S STAYING OUT AT HER SISTER'S IN WESTMONT, SO WE'VE GOT THE WHOLE PLACE TO OURSELVES.
HAVE OURSELVES A BIT OF A BOYS' NIGHT.

HEY JAMIE, DO YOU LIKE LEGOS?
YEAH.

LEGO
ASK YOUR DAD TO GO OPEN THAT TUB WHILE I GET MYSELF SOME CHILI.

IT'S...SO MANY.
LOOKS LIKE WE HIT THE JACKPOT, HUH?
YEAH.

DUMP IT ALL OUT ON THE FLOOR, IF YOU WANT. WE CAN TRY AND BUILD A CASTLE OR SOMETHING.

I WANNA BUILD A SPACESHIP.

WE COULD BUILD A CASTLE **OUT** OF SPACESHIPS.
OKAY.

I CAN'T BELIEVE YOU KEEP THIS STUFF AROUND.

I SHOULD PROBABLY PRETEND THAT I DON'T AND THAT I JUST BORROWED THE TUB FROM MY NEPHEWS.
BUT I DO LOVE SMOKING A LITTLE GRASS AND BUILDING SOME WEIRD SHIT WHILE WATCHING SOME CARTOONS.

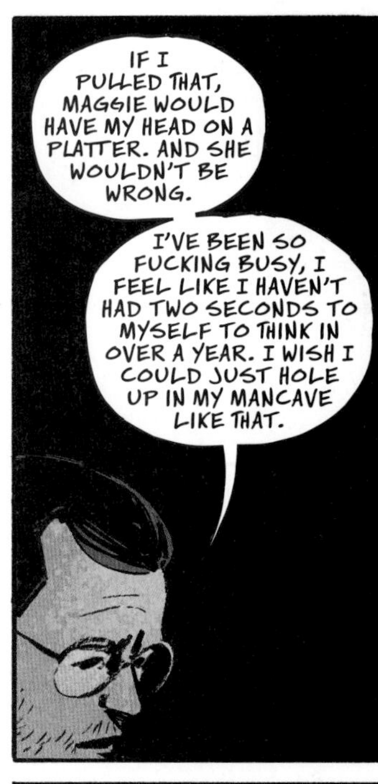
IF I PULLED THAT, MAGGIE WOULD HAVE MY HEAD ON A PLATTER. AND SHE WOULDN'T BE WRONG.
I'VE BEEN SO FUCKING BUSY, I FEEL LIKE I HAVEN'T HAD TWO SECONDS TO MYSELF TO THINK IN OVER A YEAR. I WISH I COULD JUST HOLE UP IN MY MANCAVE LIKE THAT.

JEAN'S USUALLY RIGHT BY MY SIDE WHEN I DO IT, MAN.
YOU KNOW WHAT I MEAN, THOUGH.
YOU STILL GET THE RELIEF OF IT ALL. THAT KIND OF ZEN.
I HAVEN'T FELT THAT SINCE I WAS IN MY 20S.

YOU REALLY ARE LIVING THE GOOD LIFE OUT HERE.
I DO MY BEST.

I'M SO FUCKING JEALOUS. I DON'T DO ANYTHING ANYMORE.
I CAN'T REMEMBER THE LAST MOVIE I SAW IN THEATERS, OR THE LAST LIVE SHOW I WENT OUT FOR.
YOU'VE GOT A KID.

HE'S REAL CUTE.
YEAH.
YEAH.
WHAT'S UP? YOU'RE MAKING A FACE.
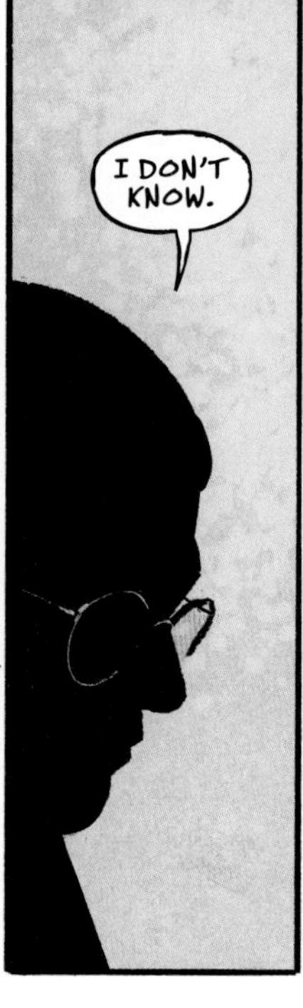
I DON'T KNOW.

WE CAN TALK WHEN THE KID'S DOWN. I'LL THROW A FEW LOGS ON THE FIRE PIT OUT BACK.
YEAH. THAT SOUNDS GREAT.

OKAY BUDDY, TIME FOR BED.

WHERE AM I TAKING HIM?
WE'VE GOT THE GUEST ROOM ALL SET UP. RIGHT THROUGH THERE.
THANKS.

DADDY?
YEAH, BUD?

I'M SCARED.

IT'S OKAY, BUDDY. IT'S NOT GOING TO GET YOU HERE. IT'S ALL THE WAY BACK IN NEW YORK.

YOU SAID...
YOU SAID I COULD SLEEP WITH YOU EVERY NIGHT...

AND I'LL BE HERE, I PROMISE.
BUT IT'S BEEN A LONG DAY, AND I HAVEN'T SEEN YOUR UNCLE MACK IN A LONG TIME.
I'M JUST GOING TO STAY UP AND TALK WITH HIM A LITTLE, THEN I'LL COME BACK TO BED.

YOU PROMISE?
YEAH. I PROMISE.

SLEEP TIGHT.

YOU YELLED AT HIM?

HE KEPT GOING ON ABOUT THIS FUCKING MONSTER.
THIS THING IN HIS CLOSET BACK IN NEW YORK AND HOW IT WAS GOING TO GET HIM.

AND THAT WAS WORTH YELLING AT HIM ABOUT?

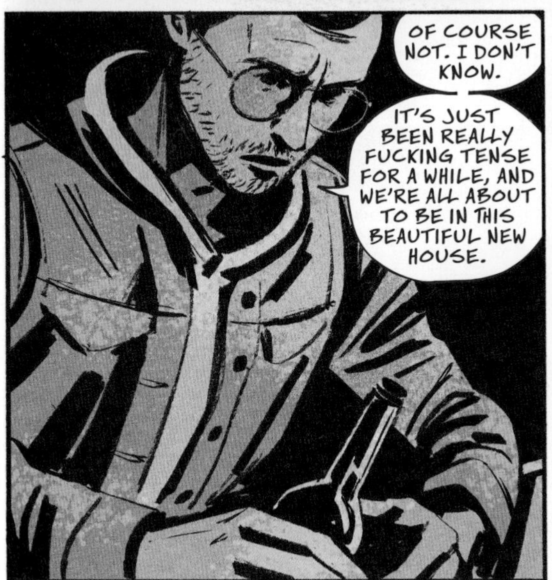
OF COURSE NOT. I DON'T KNOW.
IT'S JUST BEEN REALLY FUCKING TENSE FOR A WHILE, AND WE'RE ALL ABOUT TO BE IN THIS BEAUTIFUL NEW HOUSE.

I JUST WANT HIM TO SEE THAT WE LEFT ALL THAT BEHIND US.
I DON'T WANT HIM TO BE SCARED OF A CLOSET HE'S NEVER SEEN BEFORE, JUST BECAUSE HE **REMEMBERS** BEING SCARED OF AN OLD CLOSET HUNDREDS OF MILES AWAY.

HE'S FOUR YEARS OLD, DUDE.

I KNOW.

SO, THIS ALL MOVING-SPECIFIC, OR ARE YOU JUST THIS MUCH OF A FUCKING DISASTER IN GENERAL?
I AM THIS MUCH OF A DISASTER IN GENERAL, HAHAHAHA.

WHAT?

YOU'RE ACTING LIKE I'M JOKING. I'M NOT JOKING.

FUCK, MAN. REALLY?

YOU'RE LUCKY YOU AND JEAN DON'T HAVE KIDS. IT TAKES ALL OF THE SHITTY PARTS OF MOVING AND DIALS IT UP TO FUCKING ELEVEN.
THE LAST FEW WEEKS HAVE BEEN HELL. I'M OPERATING ON NEXT TO NO SLEEP.

I THOUGHT THIS WAS GOING TO BE, I DON'T KNOW...I THOUGHT I'D BE ABLE TO FUCKING UNWIND A BIT.

YOU DON'T *TALK* TO ME ANYMORE.
THIS IS THE ONLY CHANCE I'M GOING TO GET TO TELL YOU HOW YOU'RE FUCKING IT UP.

OKAY, SO TELL ME, THEN.

WHY ISN'T MAGGIE HERE WITH YOU?

SHE NEEDED TO GET THERE EARLY, DO HER ORIENTATION AT THE NEW AGENCY.
SO, WHY AREN'T YOU THERE WITH HER?

BECAUSE I ALWAYS WANTED TO DO THE DRIVE. WE WERE MOVING CROSS-COUNTRY. IT FELT LIKE WE SHOULD DO THE DRIVE. SO WE COULD LIKE... FEEL THE DISTANCE OF THE MOVE. MAKE IT REAL OR SOMETHING.
I TRIED TO TALK HER INTO IT. SHE DIDN'T LISTEN.

DID YOU ACTUALLY TRY OR DID YOU JUST TAKE THE CHANCE TO RUN AWAY FROM HER FOR A BIT?

COME ON, MAN. YOU'VE BEEN WITH JEAN FOR YEARS. YOU KNOW SOMETIMES IT HELPS TO GET AWAY FOR A LITTLE BIT.
TO BREATHE.

IT'S GOING TO BE SO MUCH BETTER OVER THERE. SHE'S GOT A JOB SHE'LL FINALLY BE HAPPY AT. I WON'T BE REMINDED OF ALL THE BETTER TIMES I HAD WHEN WE WERE KIDS.
YOU ALL FUCKING LEFT NEW YORK AND I GET FUCKING DEPRESSED. I KNOW THAT'S NOT FAIR TO MAGGIE OR JAMIE, BUT I CAN LEAVE THAT SHIT BEHIND ME IN A NEW PLACE.
I CAN FIND TIME TO SMOKE UP AND DO LEGOS AND WATCH CARTOONS. LIVE THE GOOD LIFE.
YOU KNOW, MAGGIE WAS A SAINT WITH HOW SHE HANDLED THAT BULLSHIT WITH MEGHAN.
DUDE, COME ON.
BUT I DON'T THINK YOU REALLY LET THAT SINK IN.
WHAT THE HELL DO YOU MEAN?

I THINK YOU'RE MAD THAT SHE DIDN'T LEAVE YOU.
IT'D BE EASIER IF SHE JUST TOOK JAMIE AND WENT TO THE OTHER END OF THE WORLD, SO YOU COULD BLAME HER FOR NOT TRYING TO FIX THINGS.
INSTEAD OF KNOWING THAT IT'S ON YOU TO MAKE THINGS BETTER. AND KNOWING THAT YOU DON'T REALLY WANT TO TRY.

COME THE FUCK ON.

LIKE I SAID. YOU DON'T CALL ME ANYMORE. SO, YOU'RE GETTING THIS ALL A BIT BLUNTER THAN I'D SAY IT OTHERWISE.

YOU'VE GOT A SMART, BEAUTIFUL, FORGIVING WIFE, AND A SWEET KID. YOU'VE GOT SOME MONEY IN YOUR BANK ACCOUNT.
YOU'VE GOT A GOOD LIFE IF YOU CAN GET OVER YOURSELF.

DUDE, YOU'RE BLOWING ALL OF THIS OUT OF PROPORTION.
YOU'RE MAKING IT SOUND LIKE...
...FUCK, MAN...

I'M DOING THE MOVE. IT WAS MY IDEA. I'M GOING ON A ROAD TRIP WITH MY KID. I'M VISITING MY FRIEND.
I WAS JUST VENTING BEFORE, YOU KNOW?

IT'S STRESSFUL TO DO A BIG MOVE, BUT IT'S A REGULAR KIND OF STRESSFUL?
IT'S NOT SOME BIG PROBLEM.

ALL THAT SHIT WAS TWO YEARS AGO ALREADY. WE'VE HAD THE FIGHTS. WE'VE DONE THE THERAPY. WE'RE REALLY GOOD. WE GO ON DATES AND SHIT. WE LAUGH.

AND IT'S JUST GOING TO GET BETTER OUT THERE.
I KNOW IT.

OKAY, I'M SORRY I OVERREACTED THEN.

IT'S OKAY.
IT'S CUTE YOU CARE.

I DO CARE. AND I'LL FLY OUT TO PORTLAND TO BEAT THE SHIT OUT OF YOU IF YOU SCREW THIS ALL UP.

GOOD. I'LL HOLD YOU TO IT.

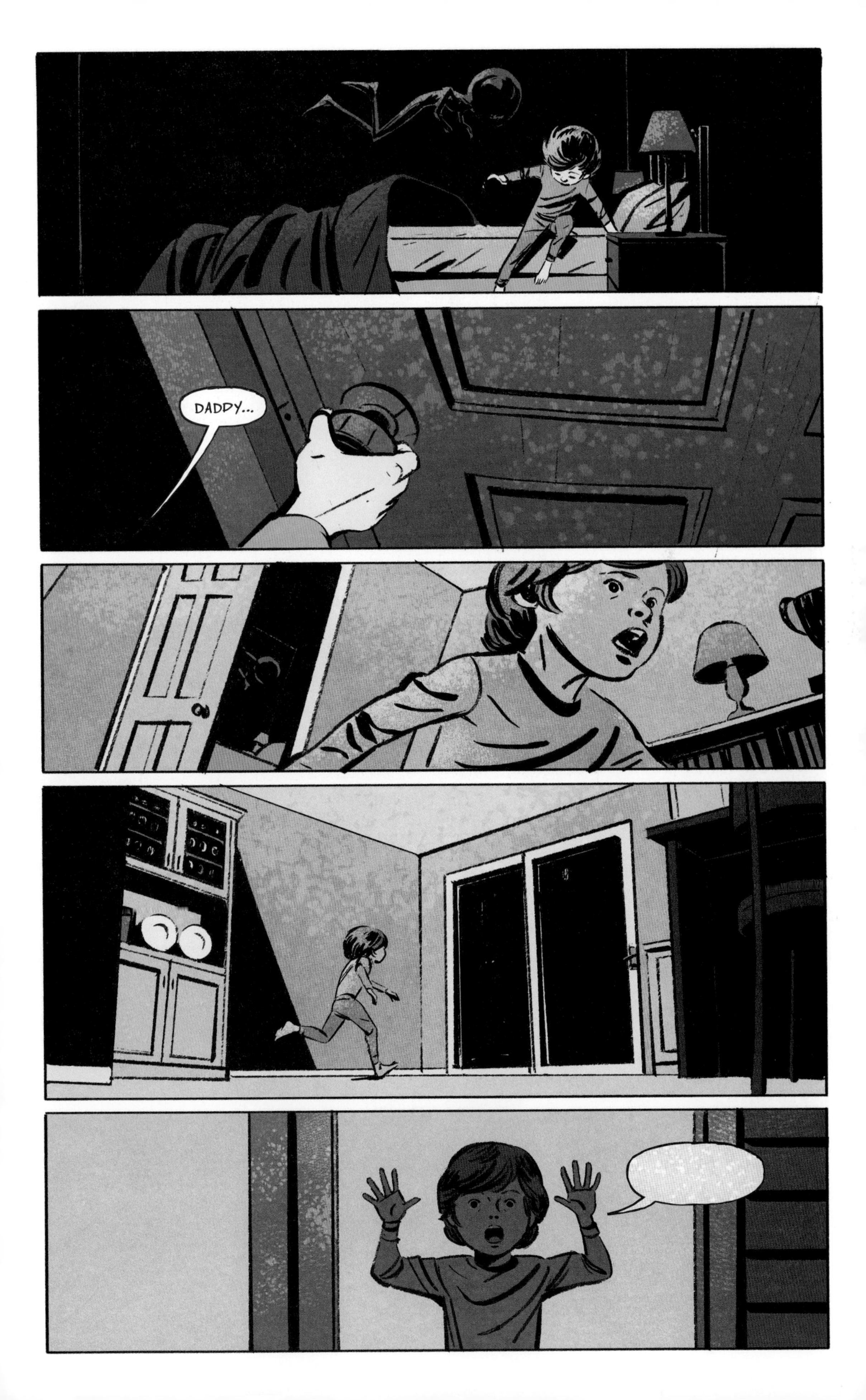
DADDY...

I FOUND A BOX OF HER STUFF WHEN WE WERE MOVING OUT.
WHOSE STUFF?

MEGHAN'S. THEY WERE THE WORST FUCKING BURNED CDS YOU EVER HEARD IN YOUR LIFE. THERE WASN'T ANY SENSE TO THE ORDER OF THE TRACKS OR ANYTHING.
BUT IT WAS NICE THAT SOMEBODY WAS THAT KIND OF...I DON'T KNOW...PUPPY DOG IN LOVE, WANTING TO MAKE MIXED TAPES.
YOU KNOW?

SOMEBODY JUST WANTING TO IMPRESS YOU, WANTING TO MAKE YOU LOVE THEM LIKE THAT.

I THINK WE SHOULD CALL IT. YOU HAVE A LONG DRIVE TOMORROW.
YEAH. GOOD IDEA.

TO BE
CONTINUED

THREE

MOT
MOTEL

CAN I BUM ONE OF THOSE OFF YOU?

YEAH, OF COURSE, MAN.

THANK YOU KINDLY.

THIS IS WHERE YOU ASK THE NICE OLD MAN WHERE HE'S COMING FROM, OR WHERE HE'S GOING, OR WHAT HIS FAVORITE FOOTBALL TEAM IS.
YEAH. NO. I KNOW. I'M SORRY.
I'M JUST IN MY HEAD.
WHAT'S A YOUNG MAN LIKE YOU HAVE TO BE IN YOUR HEAD ABOUT?
I DON'T EVEN KNOW WHERE TO START.
YOU START BY TALKING.

WE'RE MOVING OUT TO PORTLAND. MY WIFE'S ALREADY OUT THERE. I'M DRIVING OUR KID CROSS-COUNTRY.

MY DAD TOOK ME ON A TRIP LIKE THAT WHEN I WAS LITTLE. WE DID ALL THE BIG ROADSIDE ATTRACTIONS. SAW A BIG BALL OF TWINE.

I WAS BORED SHITLESS, MIND YOU, BUT I STILL REMEMBER THE FUCKING THING.

THAT SAYS SOMETHING. YOU DO SOMETHING LIKE THIS RIGHT, HE'LL HAVE SOMETHING TO HOLD ON TO FOR HIS ENTIRE LIFE.
YEAH.

WELL, WHAT IF YOU DON'T DO IT RIGHT?

WHAT'S WRONG, SON?

I'M SORRY. I'M JUST FUCKING EXHAUSTED.
I DON'T EVEN REALLY SMOKE ANYMORE BUT I JUST NEEDED AN EXCUSE TO BE OUTSIDE FOR A BIT.

AND WHY'S THAT?

HE JUST WON'T FUCKING STOP ABOUT THIS MONSTER.

MONSTER?

I'M SORRY. MY KID...HE KEEPS HAVING THESE. I DON'T KNOW. THESE NIGHTMARES.

BACK IN OUR APARTMENT IN NEW YORK, HE'D SEE THIS MONSTER COMING OUT OF HIS CLOSET AT NIGHT.

WHEN IT STARTED IT WAS ONLY EVERY COUPLE OF WEEKS, BUT RECENTLY IT'S BEEN HAPPENING ALMOST EVERY NIGHT.
AND EVERY TIME, HE'D JUST COME RUNNING INTO THE MIDDLE OF...

I DON'T KNOW. HIS MOM AND I. MAGGIE. THINGS HAVE BEEN **ROUGH,** LATELY.
EVERY NIGHT THAT I LET MY GUARD DOWN FOR HALF A FUCKING SECOND, LIKE I STOP WATCHING MYSELF, STOP PERFORMING THE PART OF THE GOOD HUSBAND...

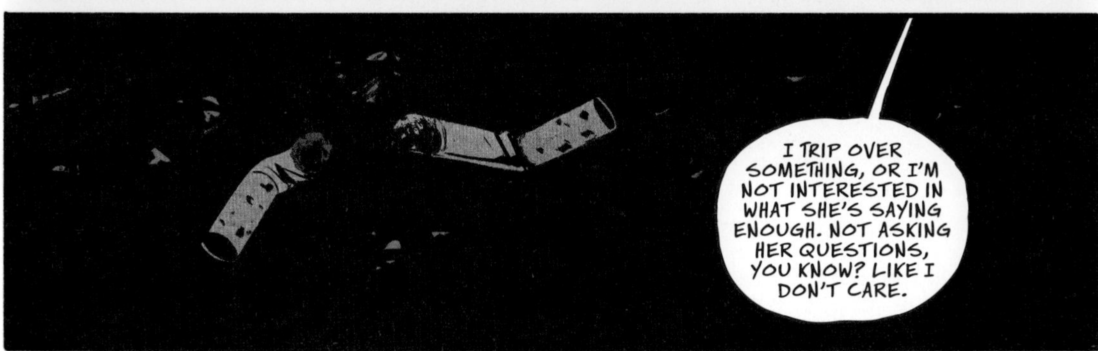
I TRIP OVER SOMETHING, OR I'M NOT INTERESTED IN WHAT SHE'S SAYING ENOUGH. NOT ASKING HER QUESTIONS, YOU KNOW? LIKE I DON'T CARE.

BUT IT'S ALL THE SAME FUCKING SHIT.
SHE'S ANGRY AT THE SAME FUCKING CO-WORKERS, AND THEY'RE DOING THE SAME FUCKING THING TO GET UNDER HER SKIN OVER AND OVER...

AND AT A CERTAIN POINT, YOU KNOW WHAT?! I'M NOT FUCKING INTERESTED. I DON'T WANT TO HEAR ANY OF THAT. I'VE HEARD IT ALL BEFORE.

I JUST WANT TO READ A BOOK, OR DICK AROUND ON MY PHONE. BUT SHE CAN **SEE** THAT, AND SHE CALLS ME OUT ON IT, AND THEN I GET UPSET...

WHICH JUST MAKES IT ALL WORSE.

AND THEN THE KID RUNS IN AND HE'S CRYING AND SCARED, AND WE HAVE TO PUT HIM BACK TO BED.

AND MAGGIE STARTS GETTING ON MY CASE ABOUT HOW I HAVEN'T MADE THE PHONE CALLS I SAID I'D MAKE, TO GET HIM HELP...

WHY DIDN'T YOU?

WHAT?
WHY DIDN'T YOU MAKE THE PHONE CALLS?

BECAUSE I KNEW WE'D BE MOVING IN JUST A FEW MONTHS, AND HE WOULDN'T HAVE THE CLOSET ANYMORE TO BE AFRAID OF.
I KNEW THAT IT'D BE OVER SOON.

BUT NOW HE'S SAYING THE MONSTER IS FOLLOWING HIM. THAT HE SAW IT AT MY FRIEND'S PLACE IN PENNSYLVANIA. THAT HE'S WORRIED IT'S GOING TO BE BACK TONIGHT.

AND YOU'RE ANGRY AT HIM FOR THAT? FOR BEING AFRAID? HOW OLD IS HE?

HE'S FOUR.

SON, IT'S NOT MY BUSINESS, BUT I DON'T THINK THIS IS ABOUT A MONSTER.

I MEAN, NO. OF COURSE NOT.
I KNOW HOW IT STARTED.

WANT A BEER?
I'LL HAVE ANOTHER SMOKE IF THAT'S WHAT WE'RE DOING.

OF COURSE.

I WAS THE STAY-AT-HOME DAD. SO, I WAS IN CHARGE OF ALL OF THE BABY SHIT WHILE MY WIFE WENT BACK TO HER OFFICE JOB.

THERE WAS THIS BABYSITTER IN THE PARK WHERE I WALKED HIM, AND WE'D LAUGH AND JOKE.

THEN ONE NIGHT I GRABBED A DRINK WITH HER. AND THEN IT BECAME WEEKLY DRINKS.
THEN IT BECAME SOMETHING MORE.

AND IT WAS SO DUMB. IT WASN'T EVEN THAT I WAS UNHAPPY.
I THINK I JUST WANTED TO KNOW THAT SOMEONE YOUNG AND BEAUTIFUL STILL WANTED ME, YOU KNOW?

SHE'D MAKE ME THESE DUMB LITTLE MIXTAPES AND WRITE ME LETTERS. AND THERE WERE PICTURES. LIKE ACTUAL POLAROIDS.
AND I WOULD HIDE THAT SHIT FROM MY WIFE, RIGHT?

I'D TUCK THEM AWAY IN THE CORNER OF MY KID'S CLOSET WHERE I KNEW SHE NEVER LOOKED. BUT THEN AFTER SHE WAS ASLEEP, I'D GO DIG THEM OUT.

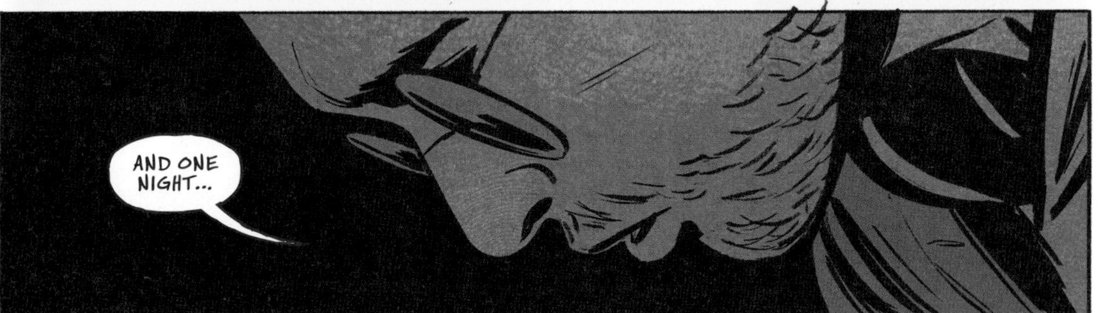
AND ONE NIGHT...

HEY! HEY, JAMIE. IT'S OKAY.

I SAW...I SAW A MONSTER.
NO.

I DID.

THERE WASN'T A MONSTER. IT'S JUST A NIGHTMARE.

WHAT'S WRONG?

HE HAD A NIGHTMARE. HE SAW A MONSTER.
OH, HONEY.

MAYBE HE CAN COME SLEEP IN OUR BED TONIGHT?
YEAH, OF COURSE.

I'VE GOT YOU, BUDDY.

HEY, THOM...
WHAT IS ALL THIS?

THINGS GOT REALLY BAD FOR A WHILE THERE.
WE STARTED SEEING A COUPLES COUNSELOR. I BROKE THINGS OFF WITH MEGHAN.

AND THEN MAGGIE GOT THIS JOB OFFER TO GO TO THE OTHER SIDE OF THE COUNTRY, AND IT SEEMED LIKE THE PERFECT WAY TO... I DON'T KNOW.
TO GIVE US THIS FRESH START. WIPE THE SLATE CLEAN.

BUT EVEN WHEN THINGS START TO COOL BACK DOWN, HE STARTS WAKING UP IN THE MIDDLE OF THE NIGHT, SCREAMING.

AND HE JUST WON'T FUCKING **LET IT GO.** THAT STUPID FUCKING CLOSET IS ALL THE WAY BACK IN NEW YORK, AND HE'S BRINGING IT THE FUCK WITH US.

I KNOW THAT MAKES ME SOUND FUCKING HORRIBLE.

IT FEELS LIKE WE'RE ALMOST IN THE CLEAR. WE'RE GOING TO HAVE THIS FRESH START IN PORTLAND. BUT HOW CAN WE DO THAT IF HE'S JUST BRINGING IT ALL WITH HIM?

SON, I DON'T KNOW MUCH. BUT I'D SAY ONE THING I FIGURED OUT WHEN I WAS A FEW YEARS YOUNGER THAN YOU IS THAT THERE ARE NO SUCH THINGS AS FRESH STARTS.

YOU DON'T WORK THROUGH A THING, OR REMOVE IT, IT JUST STAYS THERE, METASTASIZING LIKE A CANCER.

WHICH IS A SUBJECT I ALSO KNOW QUITE A BIT ABOUT. YOU MIGHT HAVE FOUND OUT IF YOU ASKED.

I'M SORRY.

YEAH.

THANKS FOR THE SMOKE.
YEAH.
FUCK.

DADDY...

JUST GO TO BED, JAMIE. WE HAVE A LONG DRIVE TOMORROW.

Portland
10 MILES

HEY, BUDDY. WE'RE ALMOST THERE.

OKAY.

I'M SORRY... I...

I WANTED THIS TO BE A FUN ROAD TRIP. SOMETHING YOU'D REMEMBER. BUT INSTEAD I JUST KEPT GETTING ANGRY.

THAT'S NOT OKAY, JAMIE. THAT'S NOT WHO I WANT TO BE. AND I KNOW IT'S UP TO ME TO MAKE THAT CHANGE. TO BE BETTER.

IN A COUPLE OF MINUTES, YOU'RE GOING TO SEE OUR NEW HOUSE. IT'S REALLY PRETTY.
IT'S GOING TO BE A PLACE WHERE YOU'RE GOING TO HAVE LOTS OF GOOD MEMORIES.

THINGS ARE GOING TO BE DIFFERENT HERE, JAMIE.

I PROMISE YOU THAT.

MOMMY!

OH, HONEY, I MISSED YOU.

HEY. HOW WAS ORIENTATION?
IT WAS GOOD. I ACTUALLY HAVE AN OFFICE HERE.

NOT JUST A TINY ROOM PRETENDING IT'S AN OFFICE.
NOT JUST A TINY ROOM.

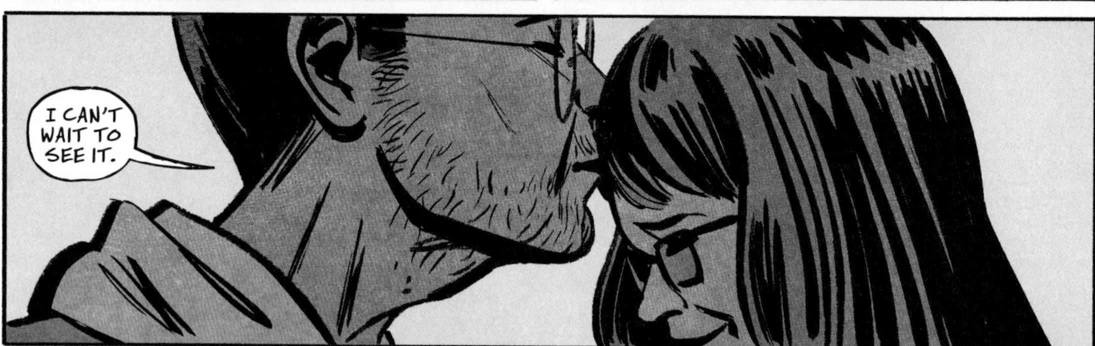
I CAN'T WAIT TO SEE IT.

DO I HAVE A ROOM?
YEAH, HONEY. JUST UP THE STAIRS.

MACK CALLED. HE SAID THAT THERE WAS SOME TROUBLE WITH JAMIE.

IT'S NOTHING. I JUST...I LET THE MOVERS PACK HIS SUITCASE, SO I DIDN'T HAVE ALL OF HIS STUFF WITH ME. IT'S FINE. HE SHOULDN'T HAVE SAID ANYTHING.

THOM, I'VE ALREADY STARTED UNPACKING. THERE WASN'T A LOOSE SUITCASE.

SHIT.

HOW MANY DAYS HAVE YOU KNOWN THIS WITHOUT CALLING ME?

REALLY. THIS IS HOW WE'RE GOING TO START OUR LIFE HERE?

CHAPTER ONE VARIANT BY **MICHAEL AVON OEMING**

CHAPTER ONE VARIANT BY **DECLAN SHALVEY**

CHAPTER TWO VARIANT BY **MICHAEL WALSH**

CHAPTER TWO VARIANT BY **FERNANDO BLANCO**

CHAPTER TWO VARIANT BY **MARTIN SIMMONDS**

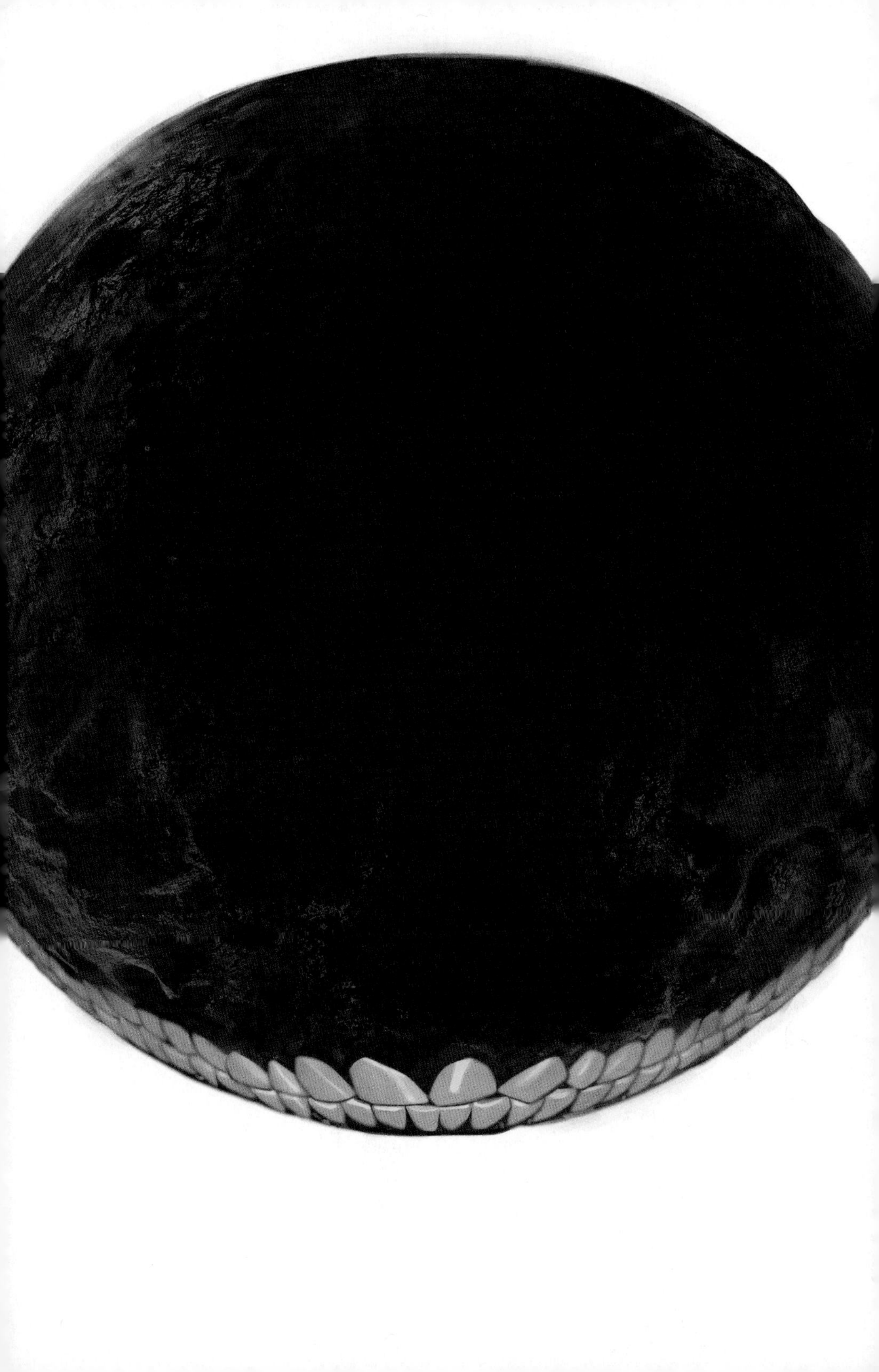

THE CLOSET

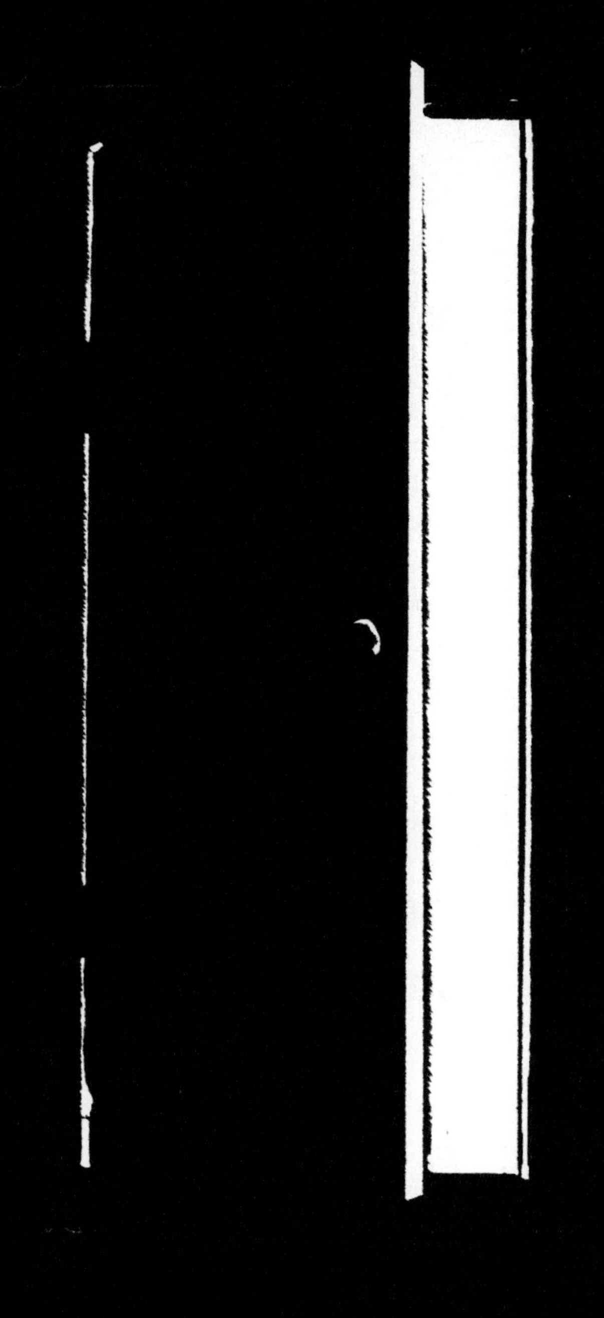

CONCEPT SKETCHES BY
GAVIN FULLERTON

LEFT CHAPTER ONE COVER SKETCH
RIGHT THOM, MAGGIE & JAMIE

CREATURE CONCEPT SKETCHES BY **GAVIN FULLERTON**

JAMES TYNION IV

IS AN EISNER AWARD-WINNING, NEW YORK TIMES BESTSELLING COMIC BOOK WRITER. HE IS THE CO-CREATOR OF *THE DEPARTMENT OF TRUTH, THE NICE HOUSE ON THE LAKE, SOMETHING IS KILLING THE CHILDREN*, AND *WYND.* HE HAS ALSO WRITTEN A LOT OF BATMAN COMICS. HE ONCE DID ONE OF THOSE DNA TESTS TO FIND OUT IF HE HAD ANY NON-IRISH ANCESTRY, AND THE TEST CONFIRMED THAT HE, IN FACT, DID NOT. HE LIVES IN BROOKLYN WITH HIS WEIRD OLD DOG.

GAVIN FULLERTON

IS A COMIC BOOK AND STORYBOARD ARTIST FROM IRELAND. HIS PREVIOUS WORK INCLUDES *BAGS (OR A STORY THEREOF)* BASED ON THE SHORT STORY BY PATRICK MCHALE AND *BOG BODIES* WITH WRITER/ARTIST DECLAN SHALVEY.

CHRIS O'HALLORAN

IS THE COMIC BOOK COLORIST FOR *ICE CREAM MAN, TIME BEFORE TIME,* AND OTHER IMAGE BOOKS AND HAS WORKED FOR MARVEL, DC, DARK HORSE, AND OTHERS. HE LIVES IN CORK CITY, IRELAND.

TOM NAPOLITANO

IS A COMIC BOOK LETTERER WHOSE BALLOONS AND ONOMATOPOEIAS HAVE APPEARED IN MANY COMICS FOR MANY PUBLISHERS SINCE 2015. HIS CREDITS CAN ALSO BE SPOTTED AS A COLORIST FOR *TALES OF THE NIGHTWATCHMAN* AND THE BACKUPS OF *SAVAGE DRAGON.* HE DOES NOT LIVE IN IRELAND BUT IS PART-IRISH PROBABLY.

DYLAN TODD

IS AN ART DIRECTOR, GRAPHIC DESIGNER, AND ASPIRING SKELETON. HE LIVES IN A HOUSE IN THE DESERT, AMONG THE LIZARDS AND SPIDERS. SOMETIMES THE WIND BLOWS.

GREG LOCKARD

IS A WRITER AND EDITOR. HE IS EDITOR OF *BLUE BOOK, THE BONE ORCHARD MYTHOS, THE ODDLY PEDESTRIAN LIFE OF CHRISTOPHER CHAOS, LITTLE MONSTERS* AND VARIOUS OTHERS. *LIEBESTRASSE*, HIS FIRST GRAPHIC NOVEL AS WRITER AND CO-CREATOR WITH TIM FISH, IS OUT NOW.

30
EST. 1992
image